CAMI KANGAROO AND WYATT TOO

BYE-BYE BULLY

Written by Stacy C. Bauer • Illustrated by Eduardo Paj

BYE-BYE BULLY
Cami Kangaroo and Wyatt Too
Published by Hop off the Press, LLC
www.stacycbauer.com
Minneapolis, MN

Library of Congress Control Number: 9798986758442
Bauer, Stacy C. Author
Eduardo Paj Illustrator
BYE-BYE BULLY
ISBN: 979-8-9867584-4-2

JUVENILE FICTION

All inquiries of this book can be sent to the author.
For more information or to book an event, please visit www.stacycbauer.com

For my son Wyatt. You bring joy and love into the world. You make the world a better place. Keep being brave, kind and true to yourself.

It was time for recess. Wyatt and his friends ran toward the soccer field.

Chester dribbled the ball down the field.
"Chester! I'm open!" Wyatt called, sprinting ahead.
Chester passed the ball to Wyatt,
who kicked it into the goal!

Wyatt spotted his friend Lenny standing on the sideline. "Lenny! Come play with us!"

Lenny ran over, stole the ball, and pushed Wyatt out of the way! He dribbled the ball down the field and took a shot.
"YEAH! Goal!"

"Why did you do that?" Wyatt asked.
Lenny had played soccer with them lots of times,
but had never acted like this before.
"Because I felt like it." Lenny shrugged.

At dinner that night, Wyatt told his family about Lenny.
"Lenny was probably just having a bad day.
He's never done anything like that before, right?" Mom asked.
"No," Wyatt answered.
"I'm sure tomorrow will be better," Dad said.
But Wyatt wasn't so sure.
What if Lenny isn't just having a bad day?

The next day at recess, Wyatt was running down the field with the ball when someone shoved him hard from behind. As he fell, he saw Lenny dribble the ball away.

"Wyatt! Are you okay?" Chester ran over and helped him up.
"What's going on with Lenny?" Jade asked, joining them.
"Let's just go to the playground," Tyson said.

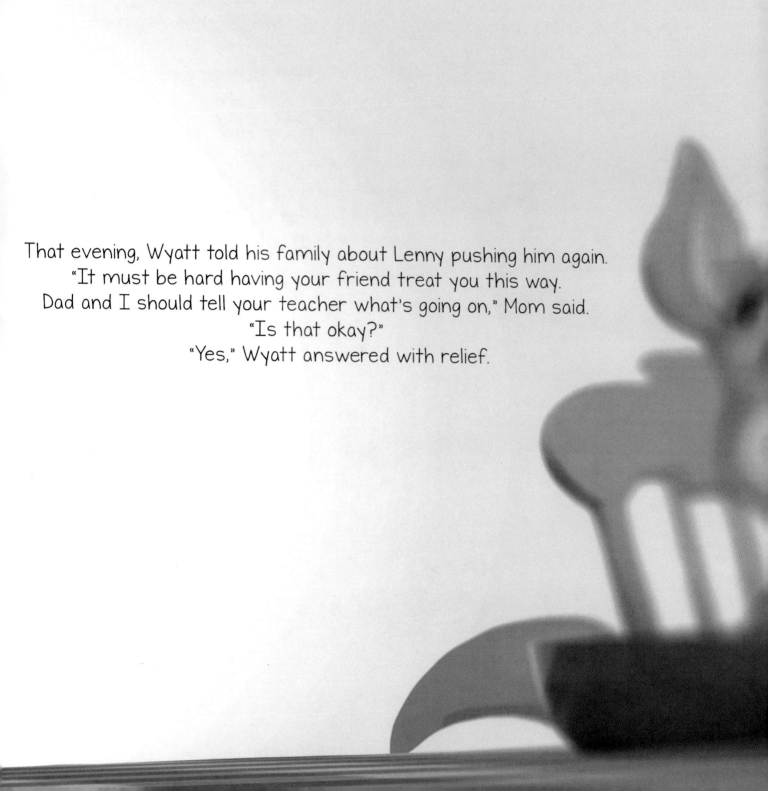

That evening, Wyatt told his family about Lenny pushing him again.
"It must be hard having your friend treat you this way.
Dad and I should tell your teacher what's going on," Mom said.
"Is that okay?"
"Yes," Wyatt answered with relief.

The next day, the teacher made Lenny sit on the bench during recess.
Wyatt and his friends had fun playing soccer.
They thought their Lenny problem was solved, but they were wrong.

Lenny knocked over Tyson's water bottle
during snack time,

laughed loudly at Chester
when he made a mistake in math class,

and tripped Jade during gym class.

When Lenny pushed Wyatt out of the line on the way back from gym class,
Wyatt told the teacher.
"Lenny, Wyatt says you pushed him in the hallway," the teacher said.
"I didn't! He's lying!" Lenny scowled at Wyatt.
"Lenny, I want you to stand at the front of the line from now on.
Wyatt, you stand back here. Both of you please keep your hands
to yourselves," the teacher said.
As soon as the teacher turned away, Lenny shot Wyatt a nasty look.
"You're such a baby!" he hissed.

At dinner that night, Cami chattered about her day while Wyatt pushed his food around with his fork.

"Is everything okay?" Dad asked later
that night. Wyatt didn't answer.
"Mom and I are here to listen. If something's
going on, we'd like to help you solve it," Dad said.
"Okay," Wyatt said. He closed his eyes
and pretended to go to sleep.

But, he lay awake for a long time.
*I thought I was doing the right thing by telling the teacher,
but maybe I shouldn't have said anything. Maybe I shouldn't have told
Mom and Dad, either. Things just seem like they're getting worse!*

The next day Lenny wasn't at school, and Wyatt's parents surprised
Wyatt and his friends with a martial arts class!
The sensei taught them deep breathing, how to be a peacemaker
and how to focus on positive thoughts.
Instead of thinking *I am such a baby*, Wyatt thought I am BRAVE.
Instead of thinking *I am WEAK*, he told himself
I am STRONG and I BELIEVE IN MYSELF.

Over the next week, Wyatt and his friends
went to martial arts every night and faced Lenny at school each day.
When Lenny knocked Wyatt's books out of his hands,
Jade and Chester picked them up.

We are KIND.

When Lenny stepped on Wyatt's heels,
he faced Lenny and told him to "STOP!" in a loud voice.

I am STRONG.

During recess, Wyatt and his friends even invited Lenny to play soccer with them!
If Lenny started being mean, they just let him have the ball and went to play something else.

We are PEACEMAKERS.

When Lenny laughed at a mistake Wyatt
made in math class,
Wyatt thought:
Everyone makes mistakes.

I BELIEVE IN MYSELF!

But, when Lenny pushed
Wyatt out of line again,
he felt frustrated.
This isn't okay.
He took a deep breath.

I am BRAVE.

"Lenny, you're being a bully.
You keep pushing us around and
calling us names!" Wyatt stated.
Jade, Chester and Tyson all agreed.
"You used to be our friend.
Why are you being so mean?"
Tyson asked.
Lenny shrank back a little and shrugged.
"We're not afraid of you and we're not
going to let you push us around anymore!"
Chester said.

They told the teacher everything.
She promised to keep a closer eye on Lenny.

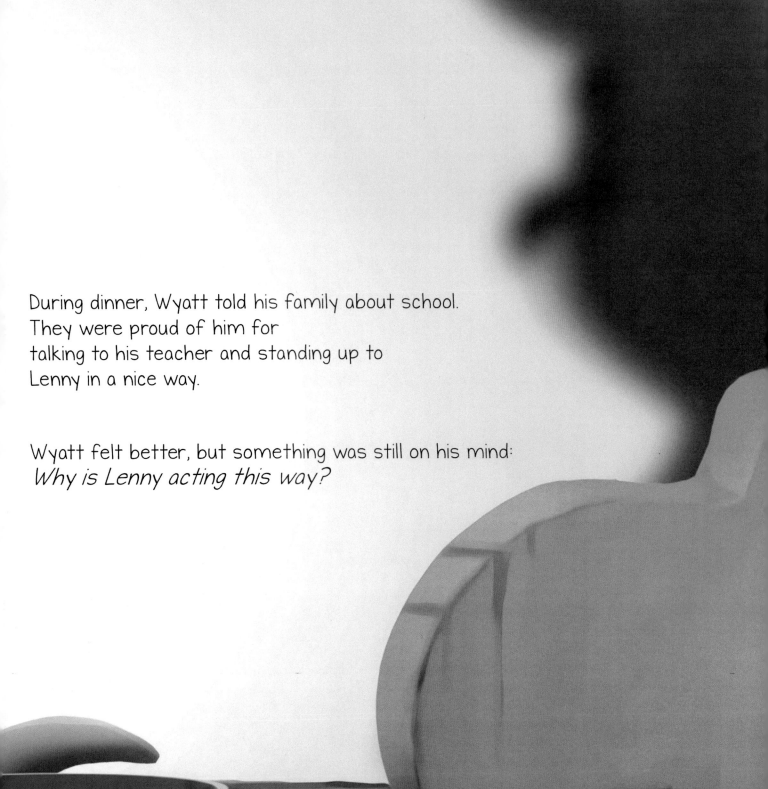

During dinner, Wyatt told his family about school.
They were proud of him for
talking to his teacher and standing up to
Lenny in a nice way.

Wyatt felt better, but something was still on his mind:
Why is Lenny acting this way?

The next day, Wyatt and his friends saw Lenny at the park with his older brother.

Lenny's brother was pushing Lenny
around the basketball court,
laughing and calling him names!

"Hey, Lenny!" Wyatt called.
"Want to play with us?"
Lenny's brother stopped,
looked up in surprise and ran off.
Jade and Chester nodded.

"Really? You want to play with me?"
Lenny asked as Wyatt helped him up.
"Sure," Tyson agreed.

On the way to the playground, Wyatt asked,
"Is your brother always like that?"
"Yeah."
"You should tell your parents."

"My dad doesn't live with us and my mom's at work all the time.
Plus, if I tell, my brother might be even worse!" Lenny said.
"I still think you should tell your mom. I was afraid to tell my parents too,
but I'm glad I did," Wyatt said.
"I'm really sorry I was so mean to you," Lenny said, sadly.
Wyatt thought for a minute.
"Do you want to come to martial arts with us tomorrow?
My parents can pick you up," Wyatt offered.

"Wyatt! I'm open!" Chester called.
Wyatt dribbled the soccer ball down the field.
He kicked the ball to Chester,
who scored.
"GOAL!"

"Can I play?" Lenny asked, hopefully.
"You can play as long as you don't cheat!"
Chester announced with a smile.
"And no pushing or tripping anyone!" Jade said.
"Okay!" Lenny smiled. "Can I be on your team, Wyatt?"
Wyatt nodded and gave Lenny a high five and a smile.
They ran toward the field to start a new game.

QUESTIONS FOR DISCUSSION:

"Because I felt like it." Lenny shrugged.
Why do you think Lenny is acting this way? What should Wyatt and his friends do?

"What's going on with Lenny?" Jade asked, joining them.
"Let's just go to the playground," Chester said.
Do you think they did the right thing by going to the playground? Should they have told a teacher at this point? Why or why not?

"Lenny, Wyatt says you pushed him in the hallway," the teacher said.
Why do you think Lenny lied to the teacher? Has someone ever lied about you to an adult? How did it make you feel? What did you do?.

As soon as the teacher turned away, Lenny shot Wyatt a nasty look. "You're such a baby!" he hissed.
How do you think Wyatt felt when Lenny called him a baby? Has anyone ever called you a name? How did it make you feel?

He closed his eyes and pretended to go to sleep.
Why do you think Wyatt chose not to tell his parents about Lenny calling him a name?

But, he lay awake for a long time.
Have you ever been so worried about something, you can't sleep? What could you do when that happens?

The next day Lenny wasn't at school, and Wyatt's parents surprised Wyatt and his friends with a martial arts class!
Why do you think Wyatt's parents signed him up for martial arts? Do you think it's a good idea?

Lenny's brother was pushing Lenny around the basketball court, laughing and calling him names!
Did it surprise you to find out that Lenny's brother was treating Lenny this way? Why or why not?

"Hey, Lenny!" Wyatt called. "Want to play with us?"
Did Wyatt do the right thing by asking Lenny to play with him?

"I'm really sorry I was so mean to you," Lenny said, sadly.
Do you understand why Lenny was mean to his friends? How should Lenny have handled his brother's treatment of him instead?

They ran toward the field to start a new game.
What do you think (or hope) will happen next for Lenny and for Wyatt?

About the Author:

Born and raised in a suburb of Minneapolis, MN, Stacy C. Bauer is a wife, teacher and mother of two. She has been writing since she was a child and loves sharing stories of her kids' antics and making people laugh. Stacy started her own publishing company, Hop Off the Press, LLC, in February of 2020 and enjoys helping aspiring authors realize their dreams. She is hoping to inspire people around the world to make a difference with her newest endeavor, nonfiction book series Young Change Makers.

About the Illustrator:

Eduardo Paj is an illustrator and graphic designer who is currently living in beautiful Mexico with his wife and two sons. Eduardo began illustrating at the age of 14 working for McGraw-Hill Education and he has continued his career creating artwork for award-winning children's books, computer games, and comics. Eduardo's images are full of life and color, and they are designed with his unique technique and versatile style.

Made in the USA
Middletown, DE
12 October 2023